JACK HUGHES

HOCKEY SUPERSTAR

BY ROY RATHBURN

Book design by Jake Nordby
Cover design by Jake Nordby

Photographs ©: Adam Hunger/AP Images, cover, 1, 4–5, 6, 30; Dave Reginek/Getty Images Sport/Getty Images, 8; Kevin Light/Getty Images Sport/Getty Images, 11, 12–13; Bruce Bennett/Getty Images Sport/Getty Images, 14; Elsa/Getty Images Sport/Getty Images, 16–17, 18–19, 27; Frank Franklin II/AP Images, 20–21; Jaylynn Nash/Getty Images Sport/Getty Images, 22; Ethan Miller/Getty Images Sport/Getty Images, 24; Red Line Editorial, 29

Press Box Books, an imprint of Press Room Editions, Inc.

ISBN
978-1-63494-872-2 (library bound)
978-1-63494-890-6 (paperback)
978-1-63494-924-8 (epub)
978-1-63494-908-8 (hosted ebook)

Library of Congress Control Number: 2023922019

Distributed by North Star Editions, Inc.
2297 Waters Drive
Mendota Heights, MN 55120
www.northstareditions.com

Printed in the United States of America
082024

About the Author

Roy Rathburn is a retired English teacher and former hockey player, coach, and official, from northern Minnesota.

TABLE OF CONTENTS

BAUER

1 THE GOAL HUNTER

Jack Hughes pounced on a bad pass. In an instant, he was one-on-one with the goaltender. The goalie went down for a block. But Hughes didn't shoot. With the puck still on his stick, he skated next to the net. Then, from behind the goal line, Hughes shot the puck. It bounced off the goalie's skate and went into the net. The crowd erupted as Hughes put the New Jersey Devils up 2–0.

In the first four years of his NHL career, Jack Hughes increased his number of goals and assists each season.

Hughes skates past hats after scoring his third goal against the Capitals.

Hughes wasn't done. Later in the period, he received a pass to the goalie's right. A Washington Capitals defender blocked Hughes's path to the net. Hughes kept his head up and picked out his target. Standing almost parallel to the side of the goal, he fired a wrist shot. The puck bounced off the goalie's mask and trickled into the goal.

In the next period, Hughes scored again. He had completed a hat trick. It was the first one of his young career. This game early in the 2022–23 season showed why the Devils were building their team around Hughes. The center had all the skills of an elite hockey player. But he also had something that can't be taught. Hughes had a goal-scorer's instinct that helped him make magic on the ice.

PAST AND PRESENT

During his hat-trick game, Jack Hughes played against Capitals left winger Alex Ovechkin. Like Hughes, Ovechkin was a star player from a young age. Hughes had beaten one of Ovechkin's records a few years earlier. He racked up 32 career points in the Under-18 World Championship, beating Ovechkin's record of 31.

USA
BAUER
BAUER
43

2 ALL-AMERICAN

Hockey has taken Jack Hughes many places in his life. He was born on May 14, 2001, in Orlando, Florida. Jack's father, Jim, was an assistant coach for the minor league Orlando Solar Bears. By the time Jack was five, Jim's coaching career had taken the family to Massachusetts, New Hampshire, and Toronto, Ontario. After that, the family stayed in Toronto for good.

Jack and his brothers, Quinn and Luke, grew up loving hockey. They learned the game from their parents. Jim had played

Jack Hughes first played for the US junior national hockey team at 16 years old.

college hockey before getting into coaching. Their mom, Ellen, was a three-sport star in college. She even played for the US women's national hockey team.

Growing up in hockey-crazy Toronto was great for Jack. The Toronto youth hockey league featured many talented players. Even in that competitive environment, Jack stood out. As the captain of his under-16 team, he tallied 58 goals and 101 assists in just 80 games.

Most Canadian players with Jack's talent would have gone on to the Ontario Hockey League. It's one of the world's best junior

A LEGENDARY TRIO

Jack Hughes was not the only talented hockey player in his family. The Vancouver Canucks drafted his older brother, Quinn, in 2018. Three years later, the New Jersey Devils drafted Jack's younger brother, Luke. All three brothers were drafted in the first round.

Jack and Quinn Hughes played together at the World Junior Hockey Championship in 2019.

hockey leagues. Jack probably would have been a top draft pick. But his American roots called him home. He decided to play for the US National Team Development Program (NTDP).

The NTDP played against American junior hockey teams and against some college teams. It also represented the United States at tournaments such as the Under-18 World Championship. So, Jack took the next step in his career while representing his country.

Jack's first major international tournament was the 2018 Under-18 World Championship. He led all players in points and assists. While helping Team USA win a silver medal, Jack was named the tournament's Most Valuable Player (MVP).

Jack starred in two seasons with the NTDP. His 228 total points were the most in program history. Jack's coaches loved his skill, competitiveness, and passion for hockey. National Hockey League (NHL) teams noticed, too.

Jack Hughes scored 74 goals in his two seasons with the NTDP.

BAUER

19

3 BEDEVILED

Many analysts thought Jack Hughes should be the top pick in the 2019 NHL Entry Draft. He had dominated at every level. And he showed all the skills needed to be a superstar in the NHL. The only knock on Hughes was his small size. He stood 5-foot-10 (178 cm) and weighed 168 pounds (76 kg).

Hughes had modeled his game after his favorite childhood player, Patrick Kane. Like Hughes, Kane was not a huge

Hughes became the eighth American to go first overall in the NHL Entry Draft when the Devils selected him in 2019.

physical presence. But with his elite skating and playmaking, he turned into one of the greatest American-born players in NHL history. Hughes wanted to follow the same path.

The New Jersey Devils took Hughes with the top pick in the 2019 draft. Not every rookie goes straight to the NHL. Some young players need more time to develop at a lower level. But Hughes made New Jersey's roster as an 18-year-old.

WHAT'S IN A NUMBER?

While playing youth hockey, Jack Hughes usually wore No. 6 on his jersey. It was a number many people in his family had worn. When the Devils drafted Hughes, captain Andy Greene already had that number. Hughes still wanted a 6 on his jersey. So, he chose No. 86, another number he'd used in his youth.

Hughes was used to dominating at each level of hockey. However, adjusting to the NHL wasn't so easy. Hughes needed eight games to score his first

Hughes (86) skates past his childhood idol Patrick Kane during a game in the 2019–20 season.

NHL goal. Fortunately, it was a memorable one. Hughes scored the only goal in a win over his brother Quinn and the Vancouver Canucks.

Hughes scored just six more goals the rest of the season. On top of his individual

86
BAUER
86
BAUER

struggles, the Devils finished in last place. But Hughes never lost confidence. He vowed to improve.

A bigger, stronger Hughes took the ice for the 2020–21 season. He added 16 pounds (7 kg) of muscle before the season started. Hughes played more minutes that year. He also had a bigger role on the team. Coaches and teammates noticed him creating scoring chances for himself and others. Even so, Hughes didn't score many goals.

Despite his slow start, Hughes earned a new contract during the 2021–22 season. It paid him $64 million over eight years. The Devils believed Hughes's breakout was just around the corner.

Hughes recorded 20 assists in his second NHL season.

GAME-WINNER

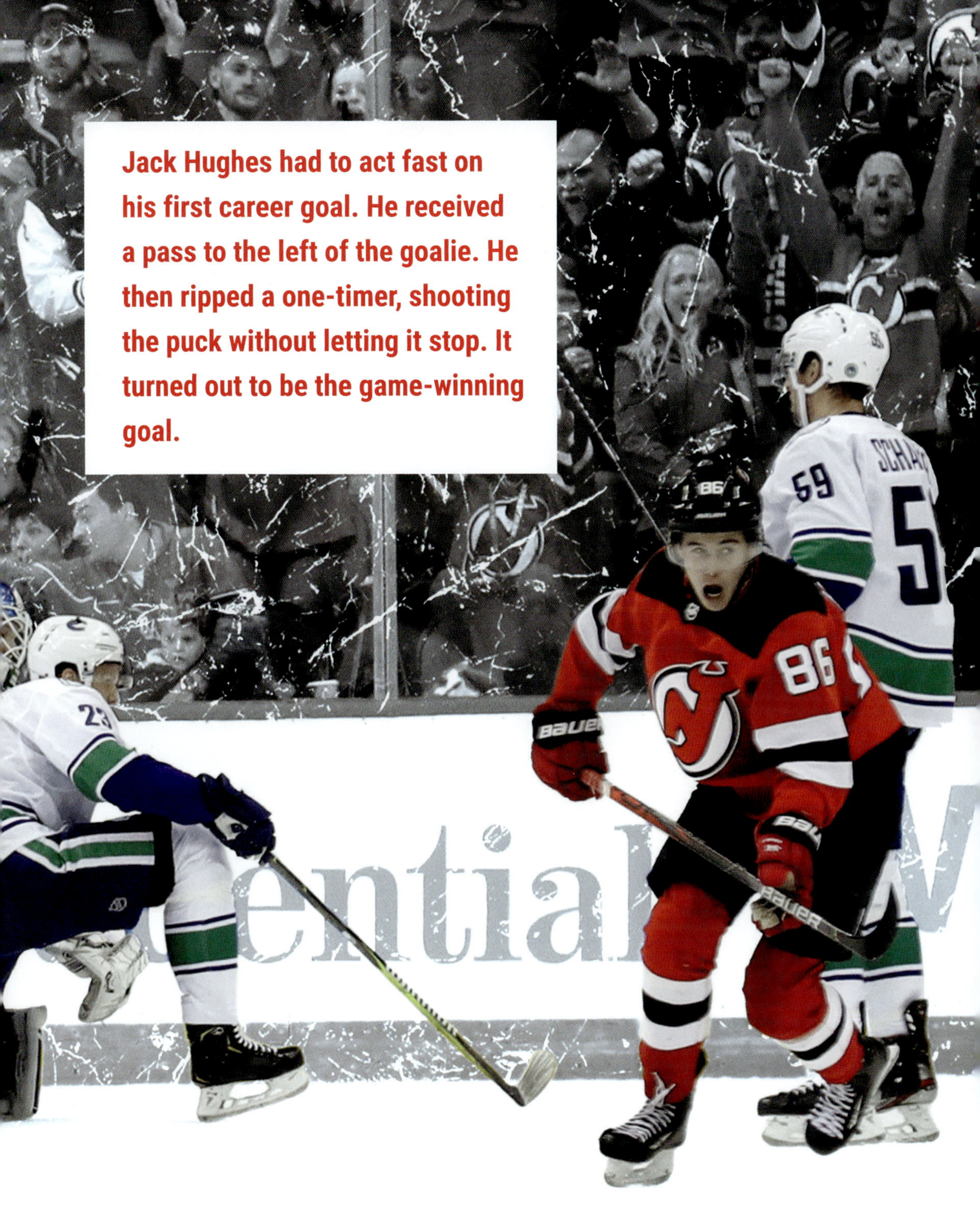

Jack Hughes had to act fast on his first career goal. He received a pass to the left of the goalie. He then ripped a one-timer, shooting the puck without letting it stop. It turned out to be the game-winning goal.

86
BAUER
GFL
Education
ottery
86
Bauer

4 THE BREAKOUT

On opening night of the 2021–22 season, Jack Hughes weaved between two Chicago Blackhawks. With just the goalie to beat, Hughes quickly shifted to his backhand. He guided the game-winning overtime goal into a wide-open net. Devils fans went crazy.

It was a perfect start to the season for Hughes. However, he suffered a shoulder injury a few days later. It was the first serious injury of his career. More of

Hughes recorded three points in the first two games of the 2021–22 season before getting injured.

Hughes competes in the Breakaway Challenge during All-Star weekend in 2022.

Hughes's magic had to wait, as he missed 17 games.

Hughes eased his way back into the lineup and soon started scoring again. He played well enough to earn a spot in that year's All-Star Game. At 20 years old, he was the youngest player in the game.

Hughes scored more goals in 2021–22 than he did in his first two years in the NHL combined. He could have scored even more. But a second injury caused him to miss the final 13 games of the season.

Health was on Hughes's side in 2022–23. By the middle of January, he had scored a career-high 27 goals. He finished the season with 43. Hughes also recorded 56 assists. His 99 points were the most in a single season in Devils history.

Behind Hughes, the Devils made the playoffs for the first time in five years. Hughes scored on a penalty shot against the New York

GIVING BACK

Jack Hughes is involved with the NHL's Hockey Fights Cancer charity program. In 2018, he led a young cancer patient in a skate around the Devils' home ice. Four years later, she and Hughes reunited for another skate. This time she was cancer-free.

Rangers for his first playoff goal. The Devils lost that game. But Hughes helped the Devils win the series in seven games.

In the second round, the Devils dropped the first two games to the Carolina Hurricanes. Back in New Jersey for Game 3, Hughes put on a show for his home fans. He assisted on the Devils' first goal and scored their second. He added a second assist and a second goal in an 8–4 win.

That was the only game of the series the Devils would win. But it was a reminder of what Hughes could do and how far he'd come. New Jersey fans couldn't wait to see what Hughes would do next.

Hughes celebrates with his teammates after scoring against the Hurricanes in a 2023 playoff game.

GEICO

TIMELINE

1. **Orlando, Florida (May 14, 2001)**
   Jack Hughes is born.

2. **Toronto, Ontario (2006)**
   The Hughes family moves to Toronto, where Jack spends most of his childhood and begins playing hockey.

3. **Chelyabinsk, Russia (April 29, 2018)**
   Hughes is named the MVP of the World Under-18 Championship and helps Team USA win the silver medal.

4. **Vancouver, British Columbia (June 21, 2019)**
   The New Jersey Devils select Hughes with the first pick in the NHL Entry Draft.

5. **Newark, New Jersey (October 19, 2019)**
   Hughes scores his first NHL goal. It's a game-winner in a 1-0 victory over his brother Quinn and the Vancouver Canucks.

6. **Paradise, Nevada (February 5, 2022)**
   Hughes plays in his first career All-Star Game.

7. **Newark, New Jersey (April 11, 2023)**
   Hughes records his 97th point of the season, setting a new Devils team record for total points in a single season.

MAP

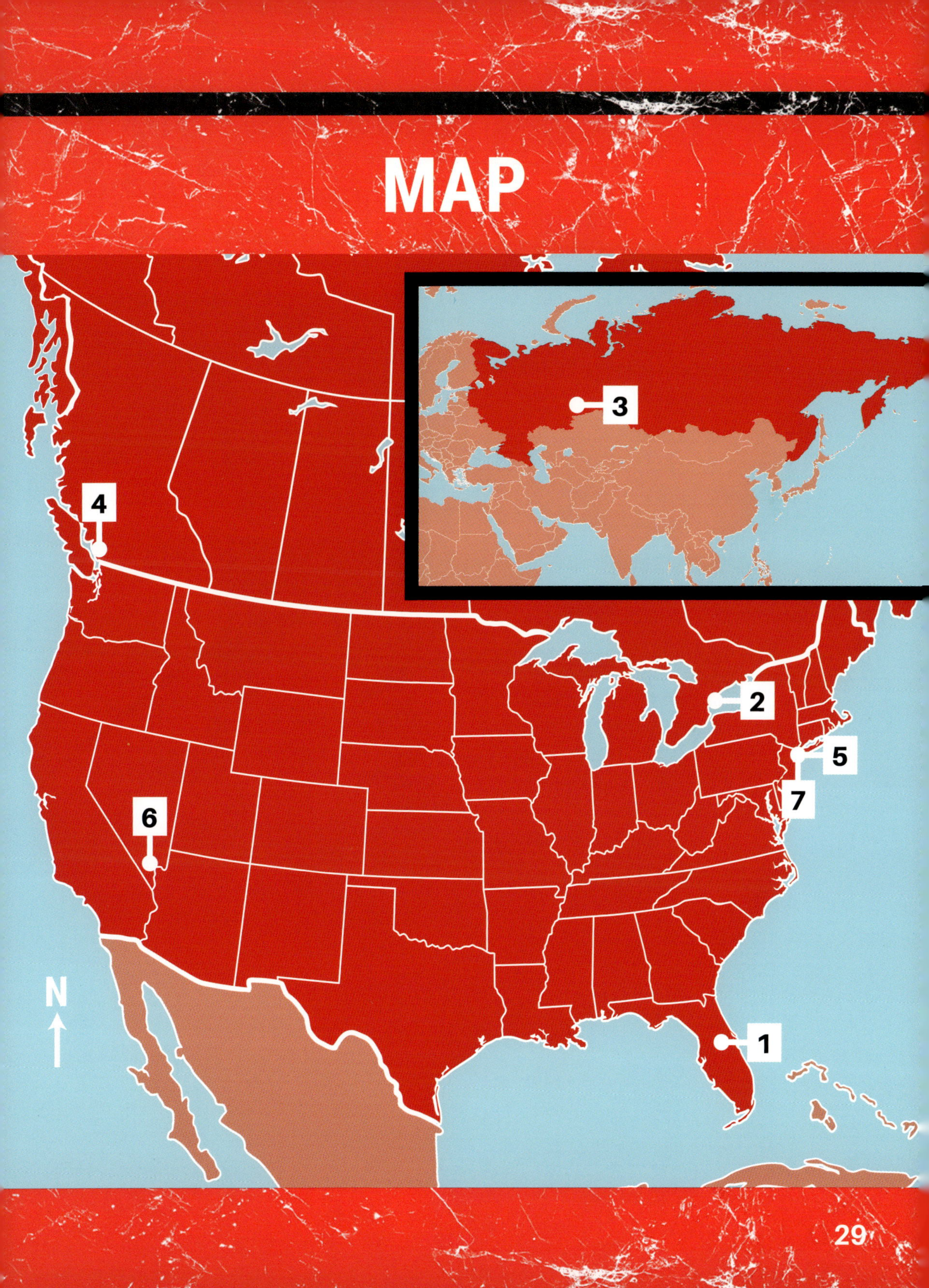

AT A GLANCE

Birth date: May 14, 2001

Birthplace: Orlando, Florida

Position: Center

Shoots: Left

Size: 5-foot-11 (180 cm), 175 pounds (79 kg)

NHL team: New Jersey Devils (2019–)

Previous team: United States National Team Development Program (2017–19)

Major awards: NHL All-Star (2022–23), World Under-18 Championship MVP (2018)

Accurate through the 2022–23 season.

GLOSSARY

analysts
People who explain the details of a game on TV.

assists
Passes, rebounds, or deflections that result in goals.

backhand
The outside of the stick blade.

captain
A player who serves as the leader of a team.

contract
A written agreement that keeps a player with a team for a certain amount of time.

draft
An event that allows teams to choose new players coming into the league.

elite
The best of the best.

hat trick
When a player scores three or more goals in a game.

junior hockey
A level of hockey in which young players can improve their skills.

playoffs
A set of games to decide a league's champion.

rookie
A first-year player.

TO LEARN MORE

Books

Berglund, Bruce. *Hockey GOATs: The Greatest Athletes of All Time*. North Mankato, MN: Capstone Press, 2024.

Hanlon, Luke. *New Jersey Devils*. Mendota Heights, MN: North Star Editions, 2024.

Wiseman, Blaine. *Stanley Cup*. New York: Lightbox Learning, 2024.

More Information

To learn more about Jack Hughes, go to **pressboxbooks.com/AllAccess.**

These links are routinely monitored and updated to provide the most current information available.

INDEX